Falling Awake:
The Remembering

Cara Johnson

 Whirling Dirvish Publishing

Published by

(◎) Whirling Dirvish Publishing

23592 Windsong, Suite 46E, Aliso Viejo, CA 92656

Text and cover design and layout
RJ Communications
51 East 42nd Street, Suite 1202
New York, New York 10017

Library of Congress Control Number: 2007929171

ISBN 13: 978-0-9768870-2-7 (paperback)

Printed in the United States of America

What follows is a remembering
of how to successfully and
consistently practice the art of
Falling Awake. Be sure when
you are reading this book that
you are someplace safe and
comfortable. Be sure to read
one page after the other.

DO NOT SKIP AHEAD.

Falling Awake

The art of Falling Awake was perfected over years and years of trial and error. This book is the first and only of its kind. Although the words may at times seem simple and the direction may not make sense, the power of this art is strong and should not be taken lightly. Follow the steps and you will remember the truth of the Dream World and the magic of Dream Traveling.

All you need to practice the art of Falling Awake is a safe and comfortable place to sit or lay down, breath, imagination and belief. All the ingredients are equally important. Do not substitute any of these, nor leave any out.

Although these words may sound simple, the effect is powerful. Remember, one of the important ingredients is belief.

Breath

Breath is the highway that connects all of life. It not only connects you to yourself, it connects you to everything and everyone. To successfully Dream Travel, you must be reminded of how to harness the power of breath.

Breath, as you know it, is not the breath of an experienced Dream Traveler. To truly breathe yourself connected is to fill your toes, your feet, your legs, your arms, your hands, your fingers, your stomach, your chest, your lungs, your heart, your neck, and your face – even your hair with breath. First, focus on slowly bringing air into your lungs and fill the bottom of your lungs first and then continue up until your entire chest is expanded. Then begin to bring air into each part of you body, starting with your toes and working your way up. Breathe air into your toes, your feet, your legs, your arms, your hands, your fingers, your stomach, your chest, your lungs, your heart, your neck, and your face – even your hair. Breathe in to each part and hold your breath. Then release your breath slowly, inch, by inch, by inch. As you breathe, feel the sensation of the breath touching every part of you until you can't feel the difference between you and not you. Slowly, inch, by inch, by inch, let your breath come in and go out until your fingers and toes tingle, and you hear a ringing in your ears.

Practice breathing in this way at least one time a day until you master the art of breath. Try not to allow yourself to fall asleep. Try to stay awake as you breathe yourself into everything in you and everything around you. Do not worry about your thoughts. As you get stronger at breathing, they will disappear.

Exercise in Breath

As you begin breathing, see your breath as a color. Whatever color you choose will work. As the breath moves into your lungs focus on filling the bottom of your lungs first and then continue up until your entire chest is expanded with breath. See your breath as color. The color should glow thru you as you breathe. Once you have filled your lungs with colored breath, focus on breathing thru your toes, your feet, your legs, your arms, your hands, your stomach, your chest, your neck, your head and your hair. Again, see your breath as color and allow yourself to glow with it. Take your time. This exercise should be taken slow and done with care.

Imagination

Imagination is at the heart of everything. Look around. Everything you see, touch, taste, hear or feel is made from imagination. It is safe to say that imagination is the force that helps create everything real and everything unreal. And it is this creative force that, when combined with breath, will allow you to Dream Travel. But, the imagination of a Dream Traveler is MUCH stronger than your average imagination. With a Dream Traveler's imagination, you not only **see** pictures in your mind, you **feel** pictures in your body. To awaken your Dream Traveler imagination, you need to practice seeing pictures in your mind. And you need to see and **feel** the pictures.

Exercise in Imagination

Lay down flat somewhere comfortable. Close your eyes. When you close your eyes start your breathing until you hear the ringing in your ears. Now, imagine the most beautiful and peaceful place in nature. Is it the beach? Is it a mountaintop? Is it the bank of a river? Is it a meadow? Pick your special place and where ever it is, imagine you are sitting, standing or laying down in this peaceful place. What do you see as you sit, stand or lay there? What is around you? What do you hear as you sit, stand or lay there? What sounds are there? What do you smell as you sit, stand or lay there? What aroma is there? What do you feel as you sit, stand or lay there? Can you feel the earth beneath you? Can you feel a soft breeze? Or maybe you can feel the spray of water on your face? What does your heart feel as you sit, stand or lay there? Do you feel peaceful, calm and happy? This is your special imagination place. Return here often and get to know your special imagination place.

Belief

The moment you say or think that you "can't" then, indeed, you can't. Believing in possibility is the beginning of remembering your connection to Belief. And it is Belief, which is the final ingredient necessary to be a Dream Traveler. Belief is the certainty that something is possible – even if it looks as though it is not possible. The sense of belief is what made it possible for us to visit the moon or create computers or even find cures for diseases. Imagination is connected to your heart and Belief is connected to your mind. The heart and mind must be reminded to work together in order to Dream Travel. To strengthen your sense of belief, you need to imagine something that you think is impossible for you to do and then imagine yourself DOING the impossible and feel your sense of Belief when you are actually DOING it.

Exercise in Belief

Any thing is possible. Anything. How do we test this? So far you have used breath to awaken your body, you have used imagination to go to your special place in nature and **feel** your special place. In this exercise, you will take it one step further and BELIEVE something that before you thought was impossible.

Start by doing your breathing exercise and once you hear the ringing in your ears, imagine an animal -- your favorite animal. See that animal in your mind. Can you see its face? Its body? Its teeth? Its tail – does it have a tail? What color is your animal? Is your animal big or small? Now, imagine that YOU are that animal. FEEL your feet as the animal's feet. FEEL your face is the animal's face. FEEL your teeth as the animal's teeth. Does your animal have hair or scales or feathers or a shell? What does your animal do? Does it run? Does it swim? Does it climb? Does it make noise? What color is your animal? See your body as the animal's body and FEEL yourself as this animal. Run or climb or swim as your animal. Now, imagine you are looking at yourself in a mirror and what is looking back is your animal's face. Do you feel its heart beating in your chest? You have become your animal. You can repeat this exercise by becoming or doing anything that is "impossible".

Dream Traveling

If you have made it this far in the book, you have remembered how to use breath to connect yourself to everything in and around you. You have also remembered how to use your imagination to see and **feel** pictures in your mind. And you have been reminded how to use your sense of belief to make the impossible possible. The art of Falling Awake is a careful combination of all these three things, and the more you practice each of these, the better you will become at Dream Traveling. At this point, you probably have some unanswered questions like – what IS it to Dream Travel? And how do you **know** when you have Dream Traveled? And how do you control **when** you Dream Travel? Let me remind you...

Dream Traveling is the ability to go anywhere and do anything while in the Dream World. While many people fall asleep at night, Dream Travelers fall awake. They are awake while they are dreaming, which means they are aware they are dreaming and wake up in their Dream World. And with their dream imagination and belief they can think themselves to any place in time and space. After remembering the ingredients of Dream Traveling, the next step is Falling Awake so you can Dream Travel.

Exercise in
Dream Traveling

While you are in bed and before you go to sleep,
begin your breathing exercise and then go to your special
imagination place. While you are in your special imagination place say clearly that you are ready to wake up in
your dreams. You can simply say, "I am ready." Continue
this exercise each night until you experience the realization while you are dreaming that you are dreaming.
Your memory is like a muscle that needs to be exercised.
Remember all the key ingredients: breath, imagination
and belief. When you say, "I am ready," you must believe
you will wake up in your dream. Although these direc-

tions may sound simple, they are very powerful.

After you have experienced the realization in your dream that you are dreaming, you are ready to go to the next level of remembering. What follows are advanced exercises in Breath, Imagination, and Belief. Take your time with these exercises and remember, you already know how to do all of these things. All you are working on is remembering.

Advanced Exercise in Breath

If breath is the highway that connects all of life, then sound is the highway that connects breath to itself. This next exercise will take your breath and your connection to breath to the next level. To complete this you will need headphones, a music player and a song that makes your heart feel very happy and peaceful. Put your headphones on, begin playing your song and as you do, start your breathing exercise only now, **feel** your breath IS the music as you breath into your toes, your feet, your legs, your arms, your hands, your stomach, your chest, your neck, your face and even your hair. Can you feel the music breathing through your body? Continue breathing

deeply until the song is finished.

Advanced Exercise in Imagination

Lay down someplace comfortable and close your eyes. Begin by doing your breathing exercise. You can breathe normally or with color or with music – it is your choice. Once you hear the ringing in your ears, imagine that you are above your body looking down on yourself. Do you see your legs? Your arms? Your face? Once you can see your body below you, imagine you are outside your house looking down on your home from the sky. What does your house look like from here? Can you see the roof? Can you see your backyard? Can you see your front yard or your car? What else can you see? Now, imagine you are looking down on your neighborhood. What can you see from high up in the sky? Is it night or day? Do you see the streets? Are there trees? Do you see your friend's house? Do you see cars moving? Now, go even higher and look down on your city? Do you see how small the houses look? Do you see lights? Do you see water? Do you see land? What can you see from this high up? Now, go even higher. Imagine you are looking down on the United States. You can see all the land and the states and everything looks so tiny. What else do you see? Now, go even higher. Imagine you are in space looking down at the planet earth. What does it look like? And what does it feel like to be that far up? Do you see stars around you? Can you see the sun? Stay a while and look around. And then, imagine you are flying back to earth and the United States and your city and your neighbor-hood and your house and then your room and then back to looking at your body. Finally, imagine you are back in your body and **feel** your feet, your legs, your arms, your hands, your stomach, your chest, your neck, your face and your hair. When you are ready, open your eyes. You can repeat this exercise many times. But each time, try to go to someplace new and see what it looks like to you.

Advanced Exercise in Belief

In order to Dream Travel to any place in time and space, you need to be able to fly. And to fly in the Dream World, you need to be able to BELIEVE you can fly. Then you need to use your mind to think yourself to places. It sounds simple, but it can be the most difficult thing to do because of your lack of belief. Remember, you were born with the knowing. All that you are doing now is remembering. In this exercise, you will be flying.

Flying

Begin by doing your breathing exercise. You can breathe or breathe with color or breathe with sound – it is your choice. Once you hear the ringing in your ears, begin to imagine yourself in your special place. And once you have arrived at your special place, say the following in your mind, "I am ready to fly." Then, while still in your special place, imagine a large open area that is still a part of your special place. It could be a large meadow, a large open beach, a large patch in the forest, a large sand dune – but it still needs to be within your special place. You may even need to walk to this area in your special place.

Once you have arrived at this large open area within your special place, take two very deep and very strong breaths of air and then begin running forward as fast as you can – feel your arms swinging, your legs moving back and forth and your feet hitting the earth beneath you – then once you have gained a good amount of speed (when you feel you can't run any faster), jump up as hard as you can and THINK yourself up. Spread your arms wide and push them back until they form a "V" – in this way your arms will almost look like the wings of a bird. FEEL yourself in the air and THINK yourself forward in flight. Now – don't get discouraged if you don't take off on your first run. You may need to try this several times. You may even get flying and then start to fall or maybe only get a few feet off the ground. If this happens – return to your breathing and begin running again. Remember. THINK yourself up. You can fly as high and as fast as you BELIEVE you can.

Advanced Exercise in Dream Traveling

So now you remember how to breathe like a Dream Traveler. You know how to breathe with color and with sound. You have also been reminded to use your incredible imagination to go to your special place and to take a short voyage above the world. And you have taken flight with your belief and reminded yourself that you are ready to wake up in your Dream World. Now you are ready for the final exercise. In this exercise you will fall awake in your Dream World and take your first Dream Traveler voyage. Before you begin this exercise, find a picture of Mt. Everest. This is the highest mountain in the world.

You can find a picture in a book or online. But study the picture or pictures of Mt. Everest until you can **see** the mountain in your mind when you close your eyes.

You Are Now Ready To Begin.

Dream
Traveling

Begin this exercise before you go to sleep at night. Begin in your bed with your eyes closed and start your breathing exercise – you can choose to breathe or breathe with color or breathe with sound. Once you hear the ringing in your ears, go to your special place. Once you are comfortably in your special place, say in your mind, "I am ready." **Feel** the truth that you are indeed ready to wake up in your dream. Now, you are going to prepare yourself to go to a specific place in your Dream World. In this exercise, you will be going to Mt Everest. While you are still in your special imagination place, **see** Mt Everest. You can do this by imagining you are holding a picture of Mt Everest in your hand and looking at it. You can do this by imagining a book in your lap and seeing Mt Everest in the book. Or you can imagine a computer or TV in your special place with a picture of Mt Everest on the screen. But **see** Mt Everest. You also need to **feel** Mt Everest. Do you see and **feel** the cold and the snow? Can you **see** the top of Mt Everest? Stand on the top of Mt Everest in your imagination and **feel** what it is to be on top of the world. Now, say to yourself in your mind. "I will dream travel to Mt Everest tonight." **Feel** the truth of that sentence. Believe. Then let the picture disappear and allow yourself to fall asleep.

Continue this exercise until you actually visit Mt Everest in your Dream World. When you visit the mountain remember all the feelings you have and the things you see. When you wake up from your dream – write down your experience in your dream journal. After you have visited Mt Everest, use this exercise to visit other places you are curious about.

Final
Message

Now you are a Dream Traveler who has remembered the magic of Falling Awake. But, you may still have some unanswered questions. Know that all the answers you seek are waiting for you in your dreams. But there is one important question that will be answered here.

Where, exactly, can you Dream Travel to?
Answer – to any time and any place near or far,
past, present or future.
Your only limitation is you.

Time and locations in time are no more than frequencies. Think of a radio. Now see the dial of the radio. Watch in your mind as the dial is moved to change the radio station. When you see a number on the radio like 100.7 –

that is a frequency and when you tune into that particular frequency you may hear rock music. You can change the frequency by moving the radio dial. When you do, you can hear another type of music. It is the same way with time and locations in time while you are in the Dream World. Every point or place in time – both backwards and forwards – has a frequency. If you wish to visit that time or place, you simply **tune in** to that frequency. How do you tune in? Think of the Internet. When you wish to find something, you go to Google or Yahoo! and type in a search word. In the Dream World – your **mind** is like Google or Yahoo! When you wish to find something, you simply use a search word in your mind and you will be taken to that frequency. You could search by a date, by a name, by a picture in your head – anything that indicates where you would like to go. You could visit two days ago or two million days ago. You could visit your best friend or you could visit an Emperor in Rome. You could visit fairies, elves, dragons or dinosaurs. You could also visit the jungle, the bottom of the ocean or Antarctica. There is no limitation backward or forward, fantasy or reality, here or there. For, the one place where, truly, anything is possible – is your dreams. The only thing that will limit you is your own imagination and your sense of belief.

You will use the same exercise to Dream Travel no matter where you have decided to go or do. Review the last lesson. Eventually, you will get so good at dream traveling that you won't have to do the entire exercise. You will merely need to think of where you want to go or what you want to experience before you fall asleep and you will wake up in the place or the dream or the experience that was in your mind before you fell asleep. Even if you are woken up in the middle of your dream, you will be able to go back to sleep and *think* yourself right back to where you were before you woke up. Of course you will need to practice to become that strong. But with focus, you will be able to go very far in the Dream World. One night you may even wake up in your dream to find you have arrived at a place you did not ask to be in and you will find or meet a person or people who are new to you. This is when you have reached the highest level of Dream Travel. At this level, you are being called into the worlds and the dreams of others who need your help and guidance.

Now is the time to discuss what you call **nightmares**. Nightmares are the most powerful teachers of the art of Falling Awake because they challenge you to recognize the illusion of reality within the Dream World. Remember – as a Dream Traveler you have complete control of your dreams. YOU are the actor, the writer and the director of your dreams. Therefore, nightmares are a reflection of your fears.

The quickest way to conquer your nightmares is by waking up within the nightmare and facing what scares you. Remember – nightmares are designed to strengthen your skills as a Dream Traveler. It is always okay to be afraid – just remember to be brave at the same time. And if you are having the same nightmare over and over – look at what is scaring you and prepare yourself **before** you fall asleep to wake up within the nightmare and face or transform what is frightening you. If you are woken up from a nightmare and you feel paralyzed with fear, start your breathing exercise, go to your special place and calm yourself. Again, remember – YOU created the nightmare so YOU can uncreate it.

Now there is one more thing. It is important to note that time that has not yet happened is an interesting place to visit in the Dream World. You find this time by traveling forward. In any given moment, there are a million possibilities of what could happen. What affects the actual experience is choice. So what you see as you travel forward could be an actual experience that has not yet come to pass OR it could be an experience that will not come to pass because different choices are made in the future moment of time. Confusing? Do not worry. Simply know that forward travel is a great adventure.

Some will say, "Is it **real**?" The answer is, "What is **real**?" Then they will say, "It is real if you can feel it, see it, hear it, taste it and smell it." Is it real when you are being chased in your dream by a twelve-headed monster who has just taken a bite out of your foot? Did you **feel** that bite? Did you **see** the scales on that monster when you turned to find out how close he was to getting you? Did you **hear** your heart beating in your chest as you ran? Did you **taste** the sweat from your face rolling into your mouth? Did you **smell** the horrible stench of that monster as he bit into you? What is real, indeed?

Let it be known that traveling in time is the most advanced stage of Dream Traveling. But the more you practice, the better you will become.

See you in your dreams.

My Falling Awake Dreams

My Falling Awake Dreams

My Falling Awake Dreams

My Falling Awake Dreams